NIGHT LANDINGS

Night

PERENNIAL LIBRARY

HARPER & ROW
PUBLISHERS, New York
CAMBRIDGE, PHILADELPHIA, SAN FRANCISCO
LONDON, MEXICO CITY,
SÃO PAULO, SINGAPORE, SYDNEY

Landings

POEMS BY
Walter McDonald

IN MEMORY

Charlie and Vera,
Riley and Faye

FIRST EDITION

Designed by Barbara DuPree Knowles

LIBRARY OF CONGRESS CATALOGING-IN-PUBLICATION DATA
McDonald, Walter.
  Night landings.
  I. Title.
PS3563.A2914N55 1989   811'.54   88-45626
ISBN 0-06-055147-X
ISBN 0-06-096331-X (pbk.)

89 90 91 92 93 CC/FG 10 9 8 7 6 5 4 3 2 1

ACKNOWLEDGMENTS

Grateful acknowledgment is made to the following publications in which these poems first appeared:

Antigonish Review (Canada): "Fences," "Harvest" (first half of "Manna International"); *Beloit Poetry Journal:* "Prairie Dog Fork of the Brazos"; *Calliope:* "Learning to Live with Nightmares," "Manna International"; *Cimarron Review:* "The Middle Years"; *College English:* "Finding My Father's Hands in Midlife"; *Confrontation:* "Building on Hardscrabble"; *CutBank:* "And Her Fans"; *Dalhousie Review* (Canada): "The Children of Saigon"; *Event* (Canada): "What We Did in the Willows"; *Fiddlehead* (Canada): "The Digs in Escondido," "Torching Grandfather's Weed Fields"; *Florida Review:* "The Mind Is a Hawk"; *Georgia Review:* "Filing System"; *Hiram Poetry Review:* "First Solo"; *Kansas Quarterly:* "Living on Open Plains"; *Literary Review:* "Bluejays in Summer"; *Memphis State Review:* "First Solo in Thunderstorms"; *Mississippi Arts & Letters:* "Ejecting from Jets"; *Mississippi Valley Review:* "After a Year in Korea," "Night Landings"; *New Southern Literary Messenger:* "All That Aches and Blesses"; *Outerbridge:* "Honky-Tonk Blues," "Owls and Uncle Bubba"; *Pequod:* "After the Rains of Saigon," "The Last Still Days in a Bunker"; *Poetry:* "Coming Home," "Losing a Boat on the Brazos," "The Songs We Fought For"; *Poetry Canada Review:* "Nights on Lake Buchanan"; *Prairie Schooner:* "Splitting Wood for Winter"; *Rubicon* (Canada): "Perpetual Motion"; *San Jose Studies:* "Hazards of Flight"; *Sewanee Review:* "Settling the Plains," "Sleeping with Strangers"; *South Dakota Review:* "Witching"; *Tar River Poetry:* "Marriage"; *Three Rivers Poetry Journal:* "Wildcatting"; *West Branch:* "The Wild Swans of Da Lat"; *Willow Springs:* "Midnight Near Pecos."

"Losing a Boat on the Brazos," "Coming Home," and "The Songs We Fought For" were first published in *Poetry,* copyright © 1987, 1988 by the Modern Poetry Association.

"Splitting Wood for Winter" is reprinted from *Prairie Schooner,* by permission of University of Nebraska Press. Copyright © 1987 by University of Nebraska Press.

Special thanks to Texas Tech University for faculty development leaves and to the National Endowment for the Arts for a fellowship, which provided the time to write these poems.

CONTENTS

Things about to Disappear

The Songs We Fought for

All That Aches and Blesses

Hazards

of Flight

NIGHT LANDINGS

In easy orbits we learned to land
night fighters by the numbers.
Line up the propeller cone a thousand feet
above the lighted runway, pitch sixty degrees
and hold it, back pressure, back pressure,
a nudge on the rudder to hold the nose up.
Roll out, trusting the darkness,
drop the landing gear and count one thousand one

one thousand two, and turn back to base,
airspeed falling, nose falling in the turn
to final, lights of the runway pulling you home
like a magnetic compass, wings rolling level
as the nose lifts, the tire-streaked runway
dim between the skimming lights, at last
the shudder of wheels scudding along on asphalt.
All by the numbers, easy.

                    The night I soloed,
red lights rolled flashing into the woods,
searching for Pennington, his third solo, a nice kid
eager for everything. What happened in those seconds
approaching the base we only guessed.
The tower controller reported granting
clearance to land, watching the T-28 approach
and pitch-out steep as it should, but it kept on
rolling in the turn until inverted

and began to dive. The controller said *Pull up!*
and Pennington, inverted, the lighted runway gone
forever, pulled up, he thought, pulled hard toward
the voice in his headset, his eyes frantic
for stars, darkness this wooded night in Georgia
on the face of the deep, the god in his ears
pleading *pull up* and Pennington obeying
with all his soul, his good right hand

bending the stick to his groin, the throttled
engine popping fire out the manifold,
the lit wings arching the tightest Split-S
he'd ever dreamed, like a pilot's inverted hand
dropping downward, the canopy suddenly
opening like a box over acres of Georgia pine,
every needle and branch and cone vivid in the light
of Pennington's eyes bursting in flames.

FLYING A PERFECT LOOP

It doesn't feel like falling
if you do it right, five hard gravities
jamming your spine. Check wingtips
equal between two horizons
sliding like a visor around your eyes.
Vertical, don't stop, back pressure
to keep it coming, breathe
from your knees, squeeze to stop blood
rushing from your brain. Sunlight
blinks rainbows in the canopy.
Swing your eyes like incense
on a chain, there's gold at the end
of all loops. When the world
opens downward like a grave,
don't worry, the sky won't disappear
forever. Hold the control stick
steady in your fist, toes
on the rudders upside down.
The earth that fills your staring eyes
is home. Dive down through skies
sliding from your grasp. Don't grab,
five steady G's will save you.
Nose coming up, *thump,*
you enter your own invisible
prop-wash where you began this loop
in thin unstable air above the earth,
the only world there is.

EJECTING FROM JETS

Holding the armrests,
I watched the sergeant
who had shot a thousand men
take aim at me and squeeze.

My skull slammed the gong
of my helmet like a weight
hammered on a midway.
Spine jammed by the ejection seat's

cannon, staring at space,
I stuck thumbs-up
down at my buddies, all of us
amazed to be alive.

Practice saves no one
but the blessed. I could have
crashed like Dawes, on takeoff,
exploded in midair

like Jones, or wallowed too low
like Kirk, trying to save it.
Ailerons wedged, he tried
nudging his F-100 down with rudders

and almost flared. Nose high,
a touch on the pedals
to bring it level,
he let the airspeed fall,

flipped between runways
and burned. We wondered
if the charge exploded
in the flames, or if, inverted,

Kirk squeezed the last controls
still working, ejected
downward like a dart.
We found his head

crushed in his helmet,
and under the burned fuselage,
the bones of his hand
squeezing the trigger like a gun.

FIRST SOLO IN THUNDERSTORMS

This was the way plain men could fly,
lashed to a cannon-ejection seat
in a jet high over Denver. A harness
held me as close as any lover,

keeping my head and helmet
from banging the canopy, bounced
like a ball in a killer thunderstorm
at night. Even controllers with radar

couldn't help me, trapped, on trial
by lightning jagged and blinding,
in thunder exploding, the buck
and crash of down drafts

more than my spars were stressed for.
Wings rip apart in wind tunnels,
and forests hold wreckage of aircraft
missing in action. Better jets

than mine had crashed in weather,
or by the heart's confusion
in a thunderstorm at night.
Flying by dials, feet firm

on the rudders, I kept the stick
and throttle steady by faith.
At night, what can flesh do
but go on fighting panic,

believing storms like our lives
have to end, that wings never
level enough could hold me,
that only a turbine was burning.

HAZARDS OF FLIGHT

We see them fold
like schools of fish
in blue waters,

starlings and cranes,
Indian pheasants
intent on mating,

ignoring death
in the fire of engines
on takeoffs and landings.

Nothing drives them away
for long, not shotguns
or nets, they wedge

in the rotors of jets
designed to fly
faster than sound.

MARRIAGE

The neighbors' dogs have howled at the last
siren and gone back to sleep.

The lights of the park switched off at midnight,
a dark garden of swings and fountains.

I hear jet-roar
far away like a waterfall.

This late at night she returns
with slow breaths, bearing vines

of the darkest grapes,
pomegranates which open soft as lips.

She knows my eyes are open
and kisses them shut so I can see.

Her fingers know the dark
corners of my mind,

her mouth repeats the mysteries,
her flesh becomes flesh.

Animals trot by outside our window
for the blessing of names.

THE WILD SWANS OF DA LAT

Near Da Lat that winter
I often saw wild swans
graceful on bomb craters
filled by the monsoon, how odd,

how beautiful below us,
so still they might be
marble mounted on pylons.
Three green canopies of jungle

hid them, unless we hovered
overhead, exposed, propellers
whop-whopping like ground fire,
the cratered clearings

tangled with vines growing back,
the swans somehow able
to find their way down
under tiered trees to breed.

THE LAST STILL DAYS IN A BUNKER

All morning we saw flames in the distance,
rockets or mortars, not bombs, which curl
and billow up like clouds. We left the door
wide open for a breath of air,
the heavy monsoon threatening Saigon

like a flood, the only breeze
the secret files we fanned our faces with,
and shredded. I shook my head at our schemes
and sweat flew. For weeks, rockets
had fallen on the base like Sodom.

Secretaries slept nude in this walk-in vault.
At dawn when we opened eight-bolt locks
we found them dressed, their torsos
outlined in sweat on the concrete.
Now, we were alone in khaki and black shoes

scuffed dull from days of shredding orders,
like trying to hide our tracks
in the jungle. We listened for news,
but all we heard piped in
were the same old country and western tunes

that kept us human. I flung cold sweat
and fed another sealed order
into the whirring shredder, wondering
how many tons of bombs we'd abandon,
how many battles we might stop.

THE CHILDREN OF SAIGON

Always at night I found them
    climbing the piles of junk burning
        on the base. Around a flat track

I ran for miles, tight muscles
    jogging past bleachers
        where French soldiers

in parades for years
    passed out in the sun. Children
        climbed those bulldozed heaps

for food, for clothes, for trash
    piled up to blaze. I saw them
        crawling the last flare of the sun

spangled on garbage, the dump
    blazing in the sweat and blink
        of my eyes, children and old men

ragged and golden, clawing
    through flames long after sundown,
        no matter how many nights

I went without supper,
    how many leftovers I begged
        and carried in darkness

out past the tarmac and bleachers,
   passing it all to children
      who grabbed it and backed away.

Building on

Hardscrabble

BUILDING ON HARDSCRABBLE

Chopping down dense mesquites
was not enough. Every other step
was cactus, eighty flat acres
and a lake lapping one corner.

Kodachrome brochures
lured us miles from plumbing,
blinded by sand our first night in,
hub-deep and stranded.

Under the stars, the only sound
was buzzing, mosquitoes all night,
gas from a dammed-up lake,
a hint of skunk.

All summer, hawks glide and sidle
in vacant skies.
We sneeze bleached
yucca blossoms, hammer

and saw on hardscrabble
fit for goats. At night
the splash and battle of bass
in the shore reeds,

nothing outside our windows
but snakes making the rounds,
holding their rattles
tip up and silent.

LEARNING TO LIVE WITH NIGHTMARES

No one's responsible
for tricks the mind plays
awake or sleeping. At night,
I dream my life ends
at Saigon, but here I am,

watching my wife
make breakfast for children
who weren't born overseas.
What am I, a ghost? Safe
on this side of morning,

no rockets, I've stopped
reaching to check
for wounds, I'm reaching
to lace my shoes,
my own shoes.

AFTER THE RAINS OF SAIGON

I put back the rifle on a steel rack
stuck in adobe and dump a split log
on the fire. Nothing to do daily
but ride eighty acres of mesquite

and cactus, count cattle and goats
and keep the windmills turning. Nights,
I lie in the shack with windows wide,
my wife and daughters asleep

in cotton sheaths. My daughters sigh
and kick the sheets. Tonight
in the east, I hear thunder,
the rumble of bombs. Propped up,

I try to piece together why I'm here. Nothing
about this flat dry land is like Vietnam
but my own damned eyes and ears.
I walk on cool linoleum outside to smoke.

Lightning flashes in the east like flares.
Running, I shove the shack's back windows tight.
Crouched on the damp porch, smoking,
digging at splinters, I watch hard rain

and wonder how many calves will die tonight
by drowning, how many angels dance
in a flash flood, how many years
we'll live out here in a desert.

COMING HOME

At her age, my mother should know
I'd break her heart, tumble downhill
and break my neck. She never learns.
Soapsuds in her eyes, hands

winding themselves dry in her apron,
she hurries to the car and hugs us,
my wife first, at last her arms
choking the grandkids. They disappear

inside her spongy belly, giggling,
clutching and clinging. For days
she chases them like a nanny,
pots steaming on the stove, dinner

for kings. My father would have
slipped them peppermint sticks
the way he spoiled his own. Gone,
like the last passenger train

from the roundhouse. Nights,
while my kids play games in the garden,
I squint to make stars move
like Pullman windows that winked

on their way to Houston when I was nine,
the year my father died, when I knew
it was never my father's run
but waved anyway at the lights.

SPLITTING WOOD FOR WINTER

What we have here is smoke. Think of these logs
as smoke, and heave the ax the way I saw you
smoking bark behind the barn last Sunday.

Up and back, swing high and hit it,
don't bend your elbow like some bum
puffing a butt. Reach back and grab some fire

and smoke it. Now! See how they split?
That's how my father taught me thrust
when I was nine, the most power I'd held

in my life, two-bladed ax honed
like silver, heavier than rifles
that boomed out and knocked deer down,

but fierce, able to split imported piñon
in one thrust. Now, swinging this ax
grown lighter in my hands, I feel

the dry wood shudder, each log the same,
hot summers growing short,
the green leaves curling, snow clouds

blooming sooner every year. I teach my sons
the arc of most deflection, the way
wide thrust can slice hard wood like cheese.

One by one they lift my father's ax
and raise it back and try to guide it
like a kite. I hear some other voice

in my voice coaxing, Here, you boys,
reach back and grab some fire.
All logs are anyway is smoke.

WITCHING

The way to bring water gushing
out of stone is a secret a few old men
and women know—Moses, my Uncle Murphy
and others born to it, a priesthood
of dowsers witching water wells

with sticks. If a sycamore tree
led Zaccheus to living water,
Uncle Murphy claimed, it's sycamore for me.
I heard he brought in six wells
out of seven, one short

of perfect. False witches and prophets
rob the poor and turn young men
to scoffers. Men in their middle years
aren't sure: they wake at three or four,
crawl out of bed depressed

and doze in their easy chairs for hours,
counting the times a simple blood-pump
beats before it bursts. But wives
who've felt children come from nothing,
and children eager to believe

all things confess their faith
in witches. They believe at night,
almost asleep, release themselves
less consciously than prayer to dreams
all through the night.

THE MIND IS A HAWK

The mind is a hawk, trying to survive
on hardscrabble. Hunting, you wheel
sometimes for hours on thermals

rising from sand so dry no trees
grow native. Some days, you circle
only bones and snakeskin, the same old

cactus and mesquite. The secret
is not to give up on shadows, but glide
until nothing expects it, staring

to make a desert give up dead-still
ideas like rabbits with round eyes
and rapidly beating hearts.

FENCES

This is the rage for order on flat plains,
barbed wire cinched tight from post to post.
Acres of land each year go back to sand

and disappear. Nothing not tied down
stays home. Canadian geese fly over us
each fall, each spring, and never land.

Our steers four times a year trudge up
board ramps to slatted walls of trucks
from the slaughterhouse. Even our children

rise up like owls and fly away. Nights,
you turn for me to hold you. We pretend
we go away by writing French love notes

in dust on the headboard. At dawn, you
smooth old oil cloths over all we wrote
the night before. By dusk, the film is back,

the earth we live on, the dust our fingers
string new fences on, holding each other
one more night with loving words.

LIVING ON OPEN PLAINS

We thought we knew these flat,
flat miles by heart, mileage counters
inside us like circadian clocks.

Born to the plains, we learned landmarks
like the hollows of each other's flesh.
We gauged the wind by how deep

sand could drift, the depth of drought
by how many coyotes howled
on the horizon. Now,

four parents buried one by one,
the landscape shifts. Our children
grow away from us. This one

takes the stars, this one, the wind.
They live in cities
without flat horizons.

How does the sun set there?
Where are the coyotes, now?
Where is the sand running to?

Things about

to Disappear

THE DIGS IN ESCONDIDO

Suddenly, this skull, a girl's,
the cause of death obvious
and swift, a diamond-shaped
incision through the brain.

She fell face down, bowing
under the same tornado sky
we worship. Summers, we scrape
layers of dry caliche down through

pottery and arrowheads, hoping
for people, our picks flicking
bones of buffaloes and wolves.
Careful, we resurrect her.

What did she see, those last few
days? Alone at this lake,
those first plains people
kneeled this deep in the canyon,

nowhere to turn for water.
They may have sacrificed lame sons
to keep them safe, nothing
to cover them but skins

of whatever they could kill,
bison and deer, antelope
with pronged horns, and wolves.
On land this flat,

if they wondered about gods,
when they stumbled on this canyon,
they believed: a spring-fed stream,
rabbits and quail, enough flint

for fire and arrows. On some days
they felt nothing threatening, not even
wind riffling through feathers
of an arrow about to kill.

She is a bowl, a little skull.
We stroke and photograph,
and probe the flint of an arrow
trapped by the brain's hard dust.

SETTLING THE PLAINS

For here and for the afterlife
they worked and sang, kept time
with hymnbooks in both hands,
old songs of God's good grace

in a land so dry they planted
cottonseeds to prove they believed
in miracles. They buried their dead
on plains with no native stones,

deep in the earth to save them
from sandstorms that pounded
daily from the west. They prayed
for rain, the sun so dry for months

they couldn't curse. Rain fell
in floods like manna twice a year.
Like Moses, they walked across
dry land and called on God

to bless them all for doubting.
They believed whatever they put
in the dirt would live if it was
God's will and the wind blew.

PRAIRIE DOG FORK OF THE BRAZOS

This stream trickles through sand
four feet below mesquite and cactus.
We could dig all day through fossils

from a million years
when this was ocean. Some years,
even water dogs dry up and die.

Hawks living on wind ride out the drought,
gliding and staring. They know in time
something hungry and heaving in burrows

will hop through a valley of dry grass
under the shade of yucca spears,
risking whatever hovers in sunlight,

and at night, something lower, slower
will slither from burrow to burrow
over the cool sands.

WILDCATTING

In the cramped cab of a pickup, we bump down
caliche canyons between mesquite and cactus,
following hunch and arroyos more than maps.

Whatever covers oil is old and barren,
dry riverbeds, patches of bone-white alkali,
outcroppings of granite,

a billion barrels ours for the drilling.
Nothing is there until we find it.
We believe in steel bits and stone

and twist our wrenches tight,
cursing the constant spinning, each twist
of the bit like love, trying it over and over.

BLUEJAYS IN SUMMER

Jays are insane in summer.
They raid each other's nests
and screech, swoop and tumble
madly away, blue flames
up ladders of air.

Pecans are saved
in top branches, too high
to harvest, an orchard of fixed
provisions. Jays gather them
like angels, dive down to our fence

with fat pecans. Paranoid, they
wedge them between pickets,
tilt back sharp beaks and tap,
and glower, jerking blue heads
like helmets. Jays swarm,

fight each other for each pecan,
swirling like crepe paper tossed
in a whirlwind, dropping the meat
in cracked shells for sparrows
hopping on the grass.

TORCHING GRANDFATHER'S
WEED FIELDS

With kerosene we burned fields
nothing but flames could save
for farming. Rabbits leaped
through flaming hoops of weeds,

hawks and scissortails
swirled whirlwinds of smoke,
flapping, diving. We heard
the roar, the crackling of thorns,

believed we heard eggs exploding.
Stones cracked, the bones of decades
burned, snakes tried to walk,
their eyes like ripe fruit bursting.

Again last night, coyotes
begged a quarter moon for food.
Out here alone for years,
Grandfather fenced out nothing,

divided his and his neighbors'
branded cattle at roundup.
Now even the neighbors are dead
and steers are raised in feed lots.

Duplexes spring up in rows
across the range. Starving armadillos
and skunks waddle in at night
by twos, the word gone out

of people up to something.
We lie awake and wonder
what to do with hardscrabble,
the land too dry to save them.

THINGS ABOUT TO DISAPPEAR

In Escondido Canyon, pronghorns the size of fawns
dip down and drink. There's no more water
for twenty miles, the next shallow canyon
on the plains. If they sense buffalo bones

diggers find each summer, thirst muzzles them.
They stare, antelopes on thin stick legs
faster than a horse can run. From the car,
we count two dozen, holding field glasses

steady as we can in cold wind gusting
from the north. Thousands of ducks fly over,
doves, geese in arrow formations, pointing the way
away. A car backfires, or a rifle. Startled,

antelopes bolt up to high ground, the flat plains
surveyed and settled. They gallop away,
they never pause, before our eyes they fade
like a legend and run for miles.

The Songs We

Fought For

WHAT WE DID IN THE WILLOWS

Flailing the leaves, we chased cicadas
from willows, storming the tree fort
each summer morning, the blunt wings
sluggish, our own sleep
ringing with cicada roar so loud
we dreamed the world was ending.

We said our dogs were dragons we tamed
and trained to save us. When we
beat the leaves, cicadas clattered down
like Valkyries, dogs leaped and crunched
thick bodies, baring their fangs
and munching, sniffing for more.

The only girls allowed were naked
between covers of magazines we smuggled
from brothers' closets. We learned
to stack lawn chairs and boxes to lift
the dogs up to our castle, the whole ramp
teetering like our schemes of glory, the dogs

scampering up into a tunnel of boys
waiting with open arms. They ran licking
and wagging, smelling in every corner,
looking down over the edge, looking away
and down again, running to lick us,
believing we boys could do anything.

In time, we all climbed down and brought
the dogs down gently as we could.
We started chasing girls like willows
every evening, our dark sleep ringing
with voices like wings, voices so thin
we dreamed the world was ending.

At feeding time, we ran out to old dogs
waiting in the yard and wagging.
We fed and left them there to dream
of forts, to bark at meter-readers
in the alley, to chase cicadas
swooping from the trees.

OWLS AND UNCLE BUBBA

Say anything you like to an owl
and he'll talk back with blinks,
and flick his head, feathers flexed,
gold and black eyes wide, puzzled
that human words are dull. Uncle Bubba

caught barn owls for years, weighed
and measured, notched their ears
and lifted them slowly, slowly on his
glove and shoved. I remember
Aunt Myrtie busy in the chicken yard,

stalking a hen for supper, shoving
two fingers between the bones
for clearance. Any gap less,
the few eggs that hen could lay
weren't worth the grain to feed her.

She'd wring, wring until the hen
flip-flapped with a thump, blood
squirting my feet if I didn't jump
squawking like chickens. That night
I'd eat fried legs and thighs

and grin at Uncle Bubba making faces
at Aunt Myrtie, his eyebrows raised,
and shaking his bushy owl head at her
he'd blink, lifting a wing
to his beard, and whisper *who? who?*

AND HER FANS

Enter rare mud, real dirt, the lady
boys my age entered on tiptoes to ogle.
She swayed, dressed in white pasties
and feathers, the only wholly

naked thing we knew. State Fair barkers
let us in for a dollar bill
and a wink, slinking inside,
sitting on the edge of chairs

by men old enough to be our daddies.
This was the body we came for,
flesh worth slopping hogs for all year long,
worth all those winter hours milking cows

for entry fees. Now let it begin,
we whistled, rubbing our eyes all over her
on stage, our only sober work all day,
drunk on the dung of swine barns

ripe in the heat of October.
Never mind the tune, the scratch
of a warped record trying to turn
with every bump and grind of our lady.

She was our hearts' burden and desire,
to hold her feathers forever, groaning,
so close to pink fingernails
we could taste them.

AFTER A YEAR IN KOREA

Old Uncle Oscar hated cold, hauled
his lean cattle early into town
to beat the snow. Daddy kept our own steers

corralled till after Christmas,
the winter market hungry for beef.
But Daddy never froze in Korea

like Uncle Oscar's friends, near the Yalu.
I didn't know till later. I thought
he was only a friendly drunk and lazy,

staying inside by his fire, or downtown
at Earl's with honky-tonk women,
sipping draft beer, picking fights

with boys my age with beards
and draft cards they threatened to burn
to provoke him. I didn't know he'd lost

his toes and fingers. I thought he wore
the gloves for show, to make him tough.
He'd end up drunk and humming tunes

with the jukebox, the same old country
and western words he learned
before they sent him overseas to freeze,

a man with two red eyes and stumps,
without a wife, always grumbling in a coat
about a country where they'd done something

awful to the weather, maybe pesticides,
the bomb, good summers short,
the winters hard, more bitter every year.

MIDNIGHT NEAR PECOS

Last night, camped in a tent in a clearing,
I heard the storm die down in time
to hear wolves running, a deer
splashing through dry stalks

of the grain field, crashing downwind
and dying, the pack claiming their right
to fields I've leased for hunting.
I felt my old pig heart grab like a fist,

wanting them all, *my deer, mine.*
I felt the hair on my neck rise up
like pig bristles. I'd gone to market
for these deer-rifle bullets and boots.

I huffed and cursed and dared any wolves
to try blowing down my tent.
I'd fire point-blank, slaughter the pack
and make deer safe for hunters like me

for years. Mad as a boar, I lay back down
and snarled and fell asleep grunting
and rooting around in the sleeping bag
for my socks, my human feet.

HONKY-TONK BLUES

Shoving another quarter home to make
jukebox stars keep singing at night
in Texas, I think of Uncle Bubba
chopping wood, heaving his bad back
to it, in town again for a weekend.

Chips flew from his ax
like high notes. Puffing, he hummed
old country tunes that kept him fed
and human, half the honky-tonk clubs
in Texas more like his home

than Lubbock. Aunt Myrtie lived alone
five months out of six, pedaling
a Singer sewing machine to stay
faithful, trying to spin gold
from cotton threads and telegrams

he wired her twice a week. Whatever
she sewed sold fast at auction
in the mall and the county fair.
Now Bubba lives alone in a trailer park
in Austin, bait for tornadoes,

his stove a butane heater he seldom
lights. He sits outside as late
as his neighbors let him, strumming,
humming old songs like a scab
he keeps picking at over and over,

no new tunes ever right
for ballads about a cruel
good-hearted woman who let down
her spun silk rope one night
and slid out of his arms forever.

Grandfather swore it would work,
and worried that dream to oblivion.
After his stroke, after he had
to sit in that rolling chair forever,
turning with one angry hand a wheel
within a wheel, around and around
in a circle, he finally gave in
and let my mother bring him home,
took over our garage for his continual
tinkering with machines like broken toys
wired back together. All day,
Grandfather took things apart
and put them back, all
the physics he owned—levers
and gears, ball bearings,
books with cracked bindings
about inventions, and cans, a hundred
cans of lubricants.
At ninety, flat on his back
except when we turned him, he lay
breathing through wrinkled
open lips, in slow motion, his eyes
wide with pain, the timing
between groans almost perfect.

THE SONGS WE FOUGHT FOR

We drank while half the stars came out for us,
Willie and Waylon, Hank and Loretta,
ours in the glow of the jukebox.

Over the laughter and smoke of local
men and women groping for their lives,
they sob-sang all we hoped to know

of lonesome love. Nothing like
songs could break a man's heart
with the draft and a war in Vietnam

drawing him closer daily. We slumped
under our Stetsons, squinting
in blue smoke layered like gunfire,

and bought pitchers of beer for women
we never hoped to marry. Each time I took
Sweet Darlin's hand and led her

onto the dance floor, I felt the world
should end like that, slow-dancing
close as we'd ever be to another in clothes,

lost in a sad, sweet fiddle-rhythm,
sliding on polished boots
and humming softly to ourselves.

All That Aches

and Blesses

FINDING MY FATHER'S HANDS
IN MIDLIFE

What enters my hand is stiff
and cold, like old leather,
rough like the hide of a bull.

So this is the fist
of my father, the fist
he struck me with, the claw

my hand turns into. Even the nails
are his, brittle and thick, beveled
when I hold them under light.

Broad fingers, puffed at the joints,
knuckles of both fists buckled,
crisscrossed with lines like scars.

I see his blood in veins here
and here, like dry Texas streams
that flow and disappear in limestone.

When I make a fist, I see his
half-moon thumb fold over four
tight fingers, a picture of family,

that big thigh-muscle shank
of his thumb something we closed on,
muscle we loved.

FIRST SOLO

I see her thumbs-up sign
go down to take the throttle.
She turns away, chin up
and urgent, flesh I have held
in these two hands. Until now,
I could have saved her.

Rolling, the Cessna gathers
faster down the runway, leans back nose-up
and lifts. Light shimmers between her
and the earth. The wings bounce
through bumpy air. I feel my spine like hers
slam down into the seat.

Was it enough, what I gave her,
the dual hours, the time in bed
rehearsing with our hands,
the emergency steps we drilled together?
If something should ever happen to me,
I said, be able to land,

then worry about a doctor.
And she was willing,
bouncing her first dual landing,
ballooning to fifty feet and stalling
before she eased it down.
She banks, now, gear down,

falling in a turn
toward final. Nothing I can do
on this hot day but curse the pheasants
nesting in fields north of the runway
and pray they have grain enough
to stay clear of traffic.

Bring the nose down, down,
don't reach, believe the glide
will hold you, the nose rise in the flare—
There! her wheels touch, lovely,
and faster and faster, she's off again
into the sun, the wild blue.

NIGHTS ON LAKE BUCHANAN

We row to the reeds we tried at dawn
and ship the oars,
coasting through lily pads like foam.
Hands swishing the lake, we line
bone-white cypress stumps like sights.

The late sun shimmers like an oil slick.
We believe here are the ones that got away,
trophy bass to make Buchanan famous.
While water silvers, we plunk
and plunk again and reel the same

two-pounders. Knowing about hunger,
we net and save them. At dark
when bass stop jumping,
we switch surface lures to spoons,
curved steel to spin thin moonlight deep.

Now it begins, work serious as prayer,
the hard drinking. All night on our
one weekend a month trying to rescue
summer, we call up all the lures we own
and cast to every stump,

to every shadow. Drinking our last,
we curse the fast hours
reeling the dawn behind us,
gambling on one more chance to drag
fat bass spinning and flipping.

Today we understand autumn,
that easy release of breath
like good sex, when it's over.
Sleek steers are in the field,

enough stubble for months,
but they don't know it.
Now we are at peace
like cattle, the heaped grain

in the barn, the yield
good enough to feed us all
through winter, hands stiff
and raw, but healing,

and everywhere the haze
of harvested maize hangs
in a weather inversion,
a calming odor like incense.

We breathe and walk lazy
to the barn to check calves
born late in the year.
At last, for a brief while,

all is well. Even the bulls
graze head-down and silent
as if they believe this hour
goes on forever. These

are the days of plenty,
a year without locusts,
wind in the rigging of saplings
staked out and thriving.

Fat cattle are in our barns,
all fences tight,
a litter of pigs each week.
But let grain silos bulge,

the cows share stalls.
Maintain all barns
exactly as they are.
Don't tear them down

for new ones. Go look
for Lazarus at the gate.
If he is there,
invite him. If he refuses,

beg. If he dies
before we can feed him,
even our children
are doomed.

SLEEPING WITH STRANGERS

Bare boards listen to our steps like owls
and creak under us. We pause,
mounting stairs of distant relatives.
Two globed hall lights glare
from looped chains, three doors closed
like a hotel's, one door open to a commode
and a blue shower curtain drawn

as if someone waited, too shy to meet us.
All day we drove, too late to see the cousin.
Those with reason to ask identification
wrapped us in their arms like their children
returning home. Names we've known forever
bloomed into faces at the funeral home,
a family album, and strangers consoled us

as if we were the most bereaved.
At last, here in some cousin's room
we lie between stiff percale sheets,
the castered double bed a sack of feathers.
Springs sag each time we touch.
Boards groan. Trees we've never known
stare in through windowpanes all night.

ALL THAT ACHES AND BLESSES

All that aches and blesses lives in the skin,
the thinnest organ, that turtle shell we scrub
and rub the wrong way daily like brass lamps
no genies rise from to save our bones
and ashes. We wade uncovered into guilt like ice
and curse the towels that leave the same thick
hide as always. We envy snakes that shed
their skins, chameleons that translate
themselves in colorful languages.
More than the heart, we give ourselves away
in skin, the blessing over all we are.
We feel the deepest loss of fathers
not in our bones, but skin they'll never touch.

FILING SYSTEM

I have that written down, she said,
somewhere. And she always found it, though it might
take weeks, digging through stacks of brittle notes
and clippings, some bent with the corners gone.
It was all there, the unassembled diary
of her life and all she cared about—

Armistice Day, the Dionne Quintuplets,
the night Daddy fell off the ladder
and only bruised himself, the date
of her third grandchild's seventh tooth,
the night Lindbergh's child was kidnapped,
the day she saw the sun after surgery.

While Daddy lived, she stored it all in stacks
against the wall. Later, the stacks multiplied
like kittens, littered on every chair and footstool
in the house. She hobbled happily for us
and lifted them to the floor like lazy cats,
her hands inches away to make sure they balanced.

My sister bought a filing cabinet and studied
notes for months, no way to order them all—
the first time Mother gave blood in World War One
had on the back a partial list of cousins
who had died. Mother knew where the others were,
a graveyard without stones, locked in the mind

of one who had dug there for eighty years.
That cabinet stored quilts she made for children
of grandchildren she would never see.
Her last months, she could find most things
we asked about, sifting stacks we had to hand her
in her rocking chair. Sometimes her eyes

went blank. "It's here," she said, "somewhere,"
and we had no doubt it was. Later, we found
on the back of a bill the exact hour of her pain
and, in more hurried cursive, which dress to choose,
which mortuary to call. In her parlor afterwards,
not knowing what to keep and what to throw away,

we crated them all and stored them like an urn
in my sister's attic. For years
she has emptied the musty crate, keeping pictures
already faded, throwing most of the bills away.
Some day, I tell her, others will burn them all.
She smiles and goes on quietly sorting.

LOSING A BOAT ON THE BRAZOS

Downriver rocks were rapids. Believe me,
even fish have ears. Sweating, we coasted
too far out on a river we've fished
for forty years. I swear it's never
been this low, but two old cousins
can't keep the Brazos full forever.

Sharp rocks are death to aluminum boats
harder to split than wood. We're safe,
spitting out mud and minnows, but alive
after months of drought and a soaking.
Bury the boat and forget it.
We could have drowned any wet year

under tons of the Brazos flooding
downhill to the dam. We could be food
for alligator gar and catfish.
That rip is wider than the lies
we'll tell for months, the size of bass
that got away, the granddaddy cat

we finally caught that flipped
and disappeared through the hole
of the boat, going down. Let's sit
on the bank and laugh at why we let
eight hundred dollars of rods and tackle
sink and saved a shell worth less

than beer cans we crush for salvage
every day, two old fools splashing ashore,
dragging a gashed boat out
as if dry land could save it,
like old bones mired in mud we've proved
can rise and walk again.

THE MIDDLE YEARS

These are the nights we dreamed of,
snow drifting over a cabin roof
in the mountains, enough stacked wood
and meat to last a week, alone at last

in a rented A-frame, isolated,
without power, high in the San Juan.
Our children are safe as they'll ever be
seeking their fortune in cities,

our desk and calendar clear, our debts
paid until summer. The smoke of piñon
seeps back inside under almost invisible
cracks, the better to smell it. All day

we take turns holding hands and counting
the years we never believed we'd make it—
the hours of skinned knees and pleading,
diapers and teenage rage and fever

in the middle of the night, and parents
dying, and Saigon, the endless guilt
of surviving. Nights, we lie touching
for hours and listen, the silent woods

so close we can hear owls diving.
These woods are not our woods,
though we hold a key to dead pine planks
laid side by side, shiplap like a dream

that lasts, a double bed that fits us
after all these years, a blunt
front-feeding stove that gives back
temporary heat for all the logs we own.